'. . . revealing great shining fangs more than three inches long.'

PU SONGLING
Born 1640, Zibo, China
Died 1715, Zibo, China

PU IN PENGUIN CLASSICS
Strange Tales from a Chinese Studio

PU SONGLING

Wailing Ghosts

Translated by
John Minford

PENGUIN BOOKS

PENGUIN CLASSICS

UK | USA | Canada | Ireland | Australia
India | New Zealand | South Africa

Penguin Books is part of the Penguin Random House group of companies
whose addresses can be found at global.penguinrandomhouse.com.

This selection published in Penguin Classics 2015
003

Translation copyright © John Minford, 2006

The moral right of the translator has been asserted

Set in 9.5/13 pt Baskerville 10 Pro
Typeset by Jouve (UK), Milton Keynes
Printed in Great Britain by Clays Ltd, St Ives plc

A CIP catalogue record for this book is available from the British Library

ISBN: 978–0–141–39816–7

www.greenpenguin.co.uk

Contents

The Troll

Sun Taibo told me this story.

His great-grandfather, also named Sun, had been studying at Willow Gully Temple on South Mountain, and came home for the autumn wheat harvest. He only stayed at home for ten days, but when he returned to the temple and opened the door of his lodgings, he saw that the table was thick with dust and the windows laced with cobwebs. He ordered his servant to clean the place, and by evening it was in sufficiently good order for him to be able to install himself comfortably again. He dusted off the bed, spread out his quilt, closed the door and lay his head down on the pillow. Moonlight came flooding in at the window.

He tossed and turned a long while, as silence descended on the temple. Then suddenly a wind got up and he heard the main temple door flapping noisily. Thinking to himself that one of the monks must have forgotten to close it, he lay there a while in some anxiety. The wind seemed to be coming closer and closer in the direction of his quarters, and the next thing he knew the door leading into his room blew open. He was now seriously alarmed, and quite unable to compose himself. His room filled with the roaring of the wind, and he heard the sound of clomping boots gradually approaching the alcove in which his bed was situated. By now he was utterly terrified. Then the door of the alcove itself flew open, and there it was, a great troll, stooping down at first as it approached, then suddenly looming up over his bed, its head grazing the ceiling, its face dark and blotchy like an old melon rind. Its blazing eyes scanned the room, and its cavernous mouth lolled open, revealing great shining fangs more than three inches long. Its tongue flickered from side to side, and from its throat there issued a terrible rasping sound that reverberated through the room.

Sun quaked in sheer terror. Thinking quickly to himself that the beast was already too close for him to have any chance of escape and that his only hope now lay in trying to kill it, he secretly drew his dagger from beneath his pillow, concealed it in his sleeve, then swiftly drew it out and stabbed the creature in the belly. The blade made a dull thud on impact, as if it had struck a stone mortar. The enraged troll flailed out at him with its huge claws, but Sun shrank back from it. The troll only succeeded in tearing at the bedcover, and pulled it down on to the ground as it stormed out.

Sun had been dragged to the ground with the bedcover, and he lay there howling. His servant came running with a lantern, and, finding the door locked, as it usually was during the night, he broke open the window and climbed in. Appalled at the state his master was in, he helped him back to bed and heard his tale. Afterwards they examined the room together and saw that the bedcover was still caught tight between the door and the door frame. As soon as they opened the door and the cover fell free, they saw great holes in the fabric, where the beast's claws had torn at it.

When dawn broke the next morning, they dared not stay there a moment longer but packed their things and returned home. On a subsequent occasion they questioned the resident monks, but there had been no further apparition.

The Monster in the Buckwheat

An old gentleman of Changshan County, by the name of An, enjoyed working on his land. One autumn, when his buckwheat was ripe, he went to supervise the harvest, cutting it and laying it out in stacks along the sides of the fields. At that time, someone was stealing the crops in the neighbouring village, so the old gentleman asked his men to load the cut buckwheat on to a cart that very night and push it to the threshing ground by the light of the moon. He himself stayed behind to keep watch over his remaining crops, lying in the open field with spear at hand as he waited for them to return. He had just begun to doze off, when he heard the sound of feet trampling on the buckwheat stalks, making a terrific crunching noise, and suspected that it might be the thief. But when he looked up, he saw a huge monster bearing down upon him, more than ten feet tall, with red hair and a big bushy beard. Leaping up in terror, he struck out at it with all his might, and the monster gave a great howl of pain and fled into the night.

Afraid that it might reappear at any moment, An

shouldered his spear and headed home, telling his labourers, when he met them on the road, what he had seen, and warning them not to proceed any further. They were reluctant to believe him.

The next day, they were spreading out the buckwheat in the sun when suddenly they heard a strange sound in the air.

'It's the monster again!' cried old An in terror, and fled, as did all the others.

A little later that day, they gathered together again and An told them to arm themselves with bows and lie in wait. The following morning, sure enough, the monster returned a third time. They each shot several arrows at it, and it fled in fear. Then for two or three days it did not return. By now all the threshed buckwheat was safely stored in the granary, but the stalks of straw still lay higgledy-piggledy on the threshing floor. Old An gave orders for the straw to be bound together and piled into a rick, then he himself climbed up on to the rick, which was several feet high. He was treading it down firmly when suddenly he saw something in the distance.

'The monster is coming again!' he cried aghast.

Before his men could get to their bows, the creature had already jumped at him, and knocked him back on to the rick. It took a bite out of his forehead and went away again. The men climbed up and saw that a whole chunk of the old man's forehead, a piece the size of a man's palm, had been bitten off, bone and all. He had already lost consciousness, and they carried him home, where he died.

The monster was never seen again. Nobody could even agree on what sort of creature it was.

Stealing a Peach

When I was a boy, I went up to the prefectural city of Ji'nan to take an examination. It was the time of the Spring Festival, and, according to custom, on the day before the festival all the merchants of the place processed with decorated banners and drums to the provincial yamen. This procession was called Bringing in the Spring. I went with a friend to watch the fun. There was a huge crowd milling about, and ahead of us, facing each other to the right and left of the raised hall, sat four mandarins in their crimson robes. I was too young at the time to know who they were. All I was aware of was the hum of voices and the crashing noise of the drums and other instruments.

In the middle of it all, a man led a boy with long unplaited hair into the space in front of the dais and knelt on the ground. The man had two baskets suspended from a carrying pole on his shoulders and seemed to be saying something, which I could not distinguish for the din of the crowd. I only saw the mandarins smile, and immediately afterwards an attendant came down and in a loud voice ordered the man to give his performance.

'What shall I perform?' said the man, rising to his feet.

The mandarins on the dais consulted among themselves, and then the attendant inquired of the man what he could do best.

'I can make the seasons go backwards, and turn the order of nature upside down.'

The attendant reported back to the mandarins, and after a moment returned and ordered the man to produce a peach. The man assented, taking off his coat and laying it on one of his baskets, at the same time complaining loudly that they had set him a very hard task.

'The winter frost has not melted – how can I possibly produce a peach? But if I fail, their worships will surely be angry with me. Alas! Woe is me!'

The boy, who was evidently his son, reminded him that he had already agreed to perform and was under an obligation to continue. After fretting and grumbling a while, the father cried out, 'I know what we must do! Here it is still early spring and there is snow on the ground – we shall never get a peach *here*. But up in heaven, in the garden of the Queen Mother of the West, they have peaches all the year round. *There* it is eternal summer! It is *there* we must try!'

'But how are we to get up there?' asked the boy.

'I have the means,' replied his father, and immediately proceeded to take from one of his baskets a cord some dozens of feet in length. He coiled it carefully and then threw one end of it high up into the air, where it remained suspended, as if somehow caught. He continued to pay out the rope, which kept rising higher and higher until the top end of it disappeared altogether into the clouds, while the other end remained in his hands.

'Come here, boy!' he called to his son. 'I am getting too old for this sort of thing, and anyway I am too heavy, I wouldn't be able to do it. It will have to be you.'

He handed the rope to the boy.

'Climb up on this.'

The boy took the rope, but as he did so he pulled a face. 'Father, have you gone mad?' he protested. 'You want me to climb all the way up into the sky on this flimsy thing? Suppose it breaks and I fall – I'll be killed!'

'I have given these gentlemen my word,' his father pleaded, 'and there's no backing out now. Please do this, I beg of you. Bring me a peach, and I am sure we will be rewarded with a hundred taels of silver. Then I promise to get you a pretty wife.'

So his son took hold of the rope and went scrambling up it, hand over foot, like a spider running up a thread, finally disappearing out of sight and into the clouds.

There was a long interval, and then down fell a large peach, the size of a soup bowl. The delighted father presented it to the gentlemen on the dais, who passed it around and studied it carefully, unable to tell at first glance whether it was genuine or a fake. Then suddenly the rope came tumbling to the ground.

'The poor boy!' cried the father in alarm. 'He is done for! Someone up there must have cut my rope!'

The next moment something else fell to the ground, an object which was found on closer examination to be the boy's head. 'Ah me!' cried the father, weeping bitterly and holding the head up in both his hands. 'The heavenly watchman caught him stealing the peach! My son is no more!'

After that, one by one, the boy's feet, his arms and legs, and every single remaining part of his anatomy came tumbling down in a similar manner. The distraught father gathered all the pieces up and put them in one of his baskets, saying, 'This was my only son! He went with me everywhere I went. And now, at his own father's orders, he has met with this cruel fate. I must away and bury him.'

He approached the dais.

'Your peach, gentlemen,' he said, falling to his knees, 'was obtained at the cost of my boy's life. Help me, I beg you, to pay for his funeral expenses, and I will be ever grateful to you for your kindness.'

The mandarins, who had been watching the scene in utter horror and amazement, immediately collected a good purse for him. When the father had received the money and put it in his belt, he rapped on the basket.

'*Babar!*' he called out. 'Out you come now and thank the gentlemen! What are you waiting for?'

He had no sooner said this than there was a knock from within and a tousled head emerged from the basket. Out jumped the boy, and bowed to the dais. It was his son.

To this very day I have never forgotten this extraordinary performance. I later learned that this 'rope trick' was a speciality of the White Lotus sect. Surely this man must have learned it from them.

Growing Pears

A peasant was selling pears in the market. Sweet they were and fragrant – and exceedingly expensive. A Taoist monk in a tattered cap and robe came begging by the pear vendor's cart, and the man told him to be gone. When the monk lingered, the vendor began to abuse him angrily.

'But you have hundreds of pears in your cart,' returned the monk, 'and I am only asking for one. You would hardly notice it, sir. Why are you getting so angry?'

Onlookers urged the vendor to give the monk one of his less succulent pears, just to be rid of him, but the man obstinately refused. A waiter who was serving the customers at a nearby wine-stall, seeing that the scene was threatening to grow ugly, bought a pear and gave it to the monk, who bowed in thanks and turned to the assembled crowd.

'Meanness,' he declared, 'is something we monks find impossible to understand. I have some very fine pears of my own, which I should like to give you.'

'If you have such fine pears,' said one of the crowd,

'then why did you not eat them yourself? Why did you need to go begging?'

'I needed this one for the seed,' was the monk's reply.

So saying, he held the pear out in front of him and began munching it until all he had left was a single seed from its core, which he held in one hand while taking down a hoe from his shoulder and making a little hole in the ground. Here he placed the seed and covered it with earth. He now asked for some hot water to sprinkle on it, and one of the more enterprising members of the crowd went off and fetched him some from a roadside tavern. The water was scalding hot, but the monk proceeded to pour it on the ground over his seed. The crowd watched riveted, as a tiny sprout began pushing its way up through the soil, growing and growing until soon it was a fully fledged tree, complete with branches and leaves. And then it flowered and bore fruit, great big, fragrant pears. Every branch was laden with them. The monk now climbed up into the tree and began picking the pears, handing them down to the crowd as he did so. Soon every single pear on the tree had been given away. When this was done, he started hacking at the tree with his hoe, and had soon felled it. Then, shouldering the tree, branches, leaves and all, he sauntered casually off.

Now, from the very beginning of this performance, the pear vendor had been standing in the crowd, straining his neck to see what the others were seeing, quite forgetting his trade and what he had come to market for. Only

種樂

任教慳吝偏人家天道原來
是好還須刻苦開須刻實
神仙心戴譬貪頑

The water was scalding hot.

when the monk had gone did he turn and see that his own cart was empty. Then he knew that the pears the monk had just been handing out were all from his cart. And he noticed that his cart was missing one of its handles; it had been newly hacked away. The peasant flew into a rage and went in hot pursuit of the monk, following him the length of a wall, round a corner, and there was his cart-handle lying discarded on the ground. He knew at once that it had served as the monk's pear tree. As for the monk himself, he had vanished without trace, to the great amazement of the crowd.

The Golden Goblet

Yin Shidan, who rose to be President of the Board of Civil Office, was a native of Licheng who grew up in circumstances of great poverty and had shown himself to be a young man of courage and resourcefulness.

In his home town there was a large estate that had once belonged to a long-established family, a rambling property consisting of a series of pavilions and other buildings that extended over several acres. Strange apparitions had often been witnessed on the estate, with the result that it had been abandoned and allowed to go to ruin. No one was willing to live there. With time the place grew so overgrown and desolate that no one would so much as enter it even in broad daylight.

One day, Yin was drinking with some young friends of his when one of them had a bright idea.

'If one of us dares to spend a night in that haunted place,' he proposed jokingly, 'let's all stand him a dinner!'

Yin leaped up at once. 'Why, what could be easier!'

And so saying he took his sleeping mat with him and

went to the place, the others accompanying him as far as the entrance.

'We will wait here outside,' they said, smiling nervously. 'If you see anything out of the ordinary, be sure to raise the alarm.'

Yin laughed. 'If I find any ghosts or foxes, I'll catch one to show you.' And in he went.

The paths were overgrown with long grass and tangled weeds. It was the first quarter of the month, and the crescent moon gave off just enough light for him to make out the gateways and doors. He groped his way forwards until he found himself standing before the building that stood at the rear of the main compound. He climbed on to the terrace and thought it seemed a delightful place to take a little nap. The slender arc of the moon shining in the western sky seemed to hold the hills in its mouth. He sat there a long while without observing anything unusual, and began to smile to himself at the foolish rumours about the place being haunted. Spreading his mat, and choosing a stone for a pillow, he lay there gazing up at the constellations of the Cowherd and the Spinning Maid in the night sky.

By the end of the first watch, he was just beginning to doze off when he heard the patter of footsteps from below, and a servant-girl appeared, carrying a lotus-shaped lantern. The sight of Yin seemed to startle her and she made as if to flee, calling out to someone behind her, 'There's a strange-looking man here!'

'Who is it?' replied a voice.

'I don't know.'

Presently an old gentleman appeared and, approaching Yin, scrutinized him.

'Why, that is the future President Yin! He is fast asleep. We can carry on as planned. He is a broad-minded fellow and will not take offence.'

The old man led the maid on into the building, where they threw open all the doors. After a while a great many guests started arriving, and the upper rooms were as brightly lit as if it had been broad daylight.

Yin tossed and turned on the terrace where he lay. Then he sneezed. The old man, hearing that he was awake, came out and knelt down by his side.

'My daughter, sir, is being given in marriage tonight. I had no idea that Your Excellency would be here, and crave your indulgence.'

Yin rose to his feet and made the old man do likewise. 'I was not aware that a wedding was taking place tonight. I regret I have brought no gift with me.'

'Your very presence is gift enough,' replied the old man graciously, 'and will help to ward off noxious influences. Would you be so kind as to honour us further with your company now?'

Yin assented. Entering the building, he looked around him at the splendid feast that had been prepared. A woman of about forty, whom the old gentleman introduced as his wife, came out to welcome him, and Yin made her a bow. Then the sound of festive pipes was heard, and someone came rushing in, crying, 'He has arrived!'

The old man hurried out to receive his future son-in-law, and Yin remained standing where he was in expectation. After a little while, a bevy of servants bearing gauze lanterns ushered in the groom, a handsome young man of seventeen or eighteen, of a most distinguished appearance and prepossessing bearing. The old gentleman bade him pay his respects to the guest of honour, and the young man turned to Yin, whom he took to be some sort of Master of Ceremonies, and bowed to him in the appropriate fashion. Then the old man and the groom exchanged formal courtesies, and when these were completed, they took their seats. Presently a throng of finely attired serving-maids came forward, with choice wines and steaming dishes of meat. Jade bowls and golden goblets glistened on the tables. When the wine had been round several times, the old gentleman dispatched one of the maids to summon the bride. The maid departed on her errand, but when she had been gone a long while and still there was no sign of his daughter, the old man himself eventually rose from his seat and, lifting the portière, went into the inner apartments to chivvy her along. At last several maids and serving-women ushered in the bride, to the sound of tinkling jade pendants, and the scent of musk and orchid wafted through the room. Obedient to her father's instructions, she curtseyed to the senior guests and then took her seat by her mother's side. Yin could see from a glance that beneath the kingfisher-feather ornaments she was a young woman of extraordinary beauty.

They were drinking from large goblets of solid gold, each of which held well over a pint, and Yin thought to himself that one of these would be an ideal proof of his adventure that night. So he hid one in his sleeve, to show his friends on his return, then slumped across the table, pretending to have been overpowered by the wine.

'His Excellency is drunk,' they remarked.

A little later, Yin heard the groom take his leave, and as the pipes started up again, all the guests began trooping downstairs.

The old gentleman came to gather up his golden goblets, and noticed that one of them was missing. He searched for it to no avail. Someone suggested their sleeping guest as the culprit, but the old gentleman promptly bid him be silent, for fear that Yin might hear.

After a while, when all was still within and without, Yin rose from the table. The lamps had all been extinguished and it was dark, but the aroma of the food and the fumes of wine still lingered in the hall. As he made his way slowly out of the building, and felt inside his sleeve for the golden goblet, which was still safely hidden, the first light of dawn glimmered in the eastern sky.

He reached the entrance of the estate to find his friends still waiting outside. They had stayed there all night, in case he should try to trick them by coming out and going back in again early in the morning. He took the goblet from his sleeve and showed it to them. In utter amazement they asked him how he had come by it, whereupon he told them the whole story. They knew how poor he was, and that he was most unlikely to have owned such a valuable object himself, and so were obliged to believe him.

Some years later, Yin passed his final examination and obtained the degree of Doctor or *jinshi*, after which he was appointed to a post in Feiqiu. A wealthy gentleman of the district by the name of Zhu gave a banquet in his honour, and ordered his large golden goblets to be brought out for the occasion. They were a long time coming, and as the company waited a young servant came up and whispered something to the master of the household, who instantly flew into a rage. Presently the goblets were brought in, and Zhu urged his guests to drink. To his astonishment, Yin at once recognized the shape and pattern of the goblets as being identical with the one he had 'kept' from the fox wedding. He asked his host where they had been made.

'I had eight of them,' was the reply. 'An ancestor of mine was a high-ranking mandarin in Peking and had them made by a master goldsmith of the time. They have been in my family for generations, but it is a long while since I last had them taken out of storage. When I knew we would have the honour of your company today, I told my man to open the box, and it turns out there are only seven left! I would have suspected one of my household of stealing it, but apparently there was ten years' dust on the seals and the box was untampered with. It baffles me how this can have happened.'

'The thing must have grown wings and flown away of its own accord!' quipped Yin with a laugh. 'But seeing that you have lost an heirloom, I feel I must help you replace it. I myself have a goblet, sir, very similar to this set of yours. Allow me to make you a present of it.'

When the meal was over, he returned to his official residence, and taking out his own goblet, sent it round straightaway to Zhu's house. When he inspected it, Zhu was absolutely amazed. He went to thank Yin in person, and when he asked him where he had acquired the goblet, Yin told him the whole story.

Which all goes to show that although foxes may be capable of getting hold of objects from a very long way away, they do not hold on to them for ever.

Wailing Ghosts

At the time of the Xie Qian troubles in Shandong, the great residences of the nobility were all commandeered by the rebels. The mansion of Education Commissioner Wang Qixiang accommodated a particularly large number of them. When the government troops eventually retook the town and massacred the rebels, every porch was strewn with corpses. Blood flowed from every doorway.

When Commissioner Wang returned, he gave orders that all the corpses were to be removed from his home and the blood washed away, so that he could once more take up residence. In the days that followed, he frequently saw ghosts in broad daylight, and during the night ghostly will-o'-the-wisp flickerings of light beneath his bed. He heard the voices of ghosts wailing in various corners of the house.

One day, a young gentleman by the name of Wang Gaodi who had come to stay with the Commissioner heard a little voice crying beneath his bed, 'Gaodi! Gaodi!'

Then the voice grew louder. 'I died a cruel death!'

The voice began sobbing, and was soon joined by ghosts throughout the house.

The Commissioner himself heard it and came with his sword.

'Do you not know who I am?' he declared loudly. 'I am Education Commissioner Wang.'

The ghostly voices merely sneered at this and laughed through their noses, whereupon the Commissioner gave orders for a lengthy ritual to be immediately performed for all departed souls on land and sea, in the course of which Buddhist bonzes and Taoist priests prayed for the liberation of his supernatural tenants from their torments. That night they put out food for the ghosts, and will-o'-the-wisp lights could be seen flickering across the ground.

Now before any of these events, a gate-man, also named Wang, had fallen gravely ill, and had been lying unconscious for several days. The night of the ritual he suddenly seemed to regain consciousness, and stretched his limbs. When his wife brought him some food, he said to her, 'The Master put some food out in the courtyard – I've no idea why! Anyway I was out there eating with the others, and I've only just finished, so I'm not that hungry.'

From that day, the hauntings ceased.

Does this mean that the banging of cymbals and gongs, the beating of bells and drums, and other esoteric practices for the release of wandering souls are necessarily efficacious?

Scorched Moth the Taoist

The household of Hanlin Academician Dong was troubled by fox-spirits. Tiles, pebbles and brick shards were liable to fly around the house like hailstones at any moment, and his family and household were forever having to take shelter and wait for the disturbances to abate before they dared carry on with their daily duties. Dong himself was so affected by this state of affairs that he rented a residence belonging to Under-Secretary Sun, and moved there to avoid his troubles. But the fox-spirits merely followed him.

One day when he was on duty at court and described this strange phenomenon to his colleagues, a senior minister mentioned a certain Taoist master from the north-east by the name of Jiao Ming – Scorched Moth – who lived in the Inner Manchu City and issued exorcist spells and talismans reputed for their efficacy. Dong paid the man a personal call and requested his aid, whereupon the Master wrote out some charms in cinnabar-red ink and told Dong to paste them on his wall. The foxes were unperturbed by these measures, however, and continued to hurl things around with greater vigour than ever. Dong reported back to the Taoist, who was angered by this apparent failure of his charms and came in person to Dong's house, where he set up an altar and performed a full rite of exorcism. Suddenly they beheld a huge fox crouching on the ground before the altar. Dong's household had suffered long from this creature's antics, and the servants felt a deep-seated sense of grievance towards it. One of the maids went up to it to deal it a blow, only to fall dead to the ground.

'This is a vicious beast!' exclaimed the Taoist. 'Even I could not subdue it! This girl was very foolish to provoke it.' He continued, 'Nonetheless, we can now use *her* to question the fox.'

Pointing his index finger and middle finger at the maid, he pronounced certain spells, and suddenly she rose from the ground and knelt before him. The Taoist asked her where she hailed from.

'I come from the Western Regions,' replied the maid, in a voice that was clearly not her own but that of the fox. 'We have been here in the capital for eighteen generations.'

'How dare creatures such as you dwell in the proximity of His Imperial Majesty? Off with you at once!'

The fox-voice was silent, and the Taoist thumped the altar-table angrily. 'How dare you disobey my orders? Delay a moment longer, and my magic powers will work on you harshly!'

The fox shrank back fearfully, indicating his submission, and the Taoist urged him once more to be gone. Meanwhile the maid had fallen to the ground again, dead to the world. It was a long while before she regained consciousness.

All of a sudden they saw four or five white lumps of some strange substance go bouncing like balls one after the other along the eaves of the building, until they were all gone. Then peace finally reigned in the Dong household.

The Giant Turtle

An elderly gentleman called Zhang, a native of the western region of Jin, was about to give away his daughter in marriage, and took his family with him by boat on a trip to the South, having decided to purchase there all that was necessary for her trousseau. When the boat arrived at Gold Mountain, he went ahead across the river, leaving his family on board and warning them not to fry any strong-smelling meat during his absence, for fear of provoking the turtle-demon that lurked in the river. This vicious creature would be sure to come out if it smelled meat cooking, and would destroy the boat and eat alive anyone on board. It had been wreaking havoc in the area for a long while.

Once the old man had left, his family quite forgot his words of caution, lit a fire on deck and began to cook meat on it. All of a sudden a great wave arose, overturning their boat and drowning both Zhang's wife and daughter. When Zhang returned, he was grief-stricken at their deaths. He climbed up to the monastery on Gold Mountain and called on the monks there, asking them for information about the turtle's strange ways, so that he could plan his revenge. The monks were appalled at his intentions.

'We live with the turtle every day, in constant fear of the devastation it is capable of causing. All we can do is worship it and pray to it not to fly into a rage. From time to time we slaughter animals, cut them in half and throw them into the river. The turtle jumps out of the water, gulps them down and disappears. No one would be so crazy as to try to seek revenge!'

As he listened to the monks' words, Zhang was already forming his plan. He recruited a local blacksmith, who set up a furnace on the hillside above the river and smelted a large lump of iron, over a hundred catties in weight. Zhang then ascertained the turtle's exact hiding place and hired a number of strong men to lift up the red-hot molten iron with a great pair of tongs and hurl it into the river. True to form, the turtle leaped out of the water, gulped down the molten metal and plunged back into the river. Minutes later, mountainous waves came boiling to the water's surface. Then, in an instant, the river became calm and the turtle could be seen floating dead on the water.

Travellers and monks alike rejoiced at the turtle's death. They built a temple to old man Zhang, erected a statue of him inside it and worshipped him as a water god. When they prayed to him, their wishes were always fulfilled.

A Fatal Joke

The schoolmaster Sun Jingxia once told this story.

A certain fellow of the locality, let us call him 'X', was killed by bandits during one of their raids. His head flopped down on to his chest. When the bandits had gone and the family came to recover the corpse for burial, they detected the faintest trace of breathing, and on closer examination saw that the man's windpipe was not quite severed. A finger's breadth remained. So they carried him home, supporting the head carefully, and after a day and a night, he began to make a moaning noise. They fed him minute quantities of food with a spoon and chopsticks, and after six months he was fully recovered.

Ten years later, he was sitting talking with two or three of his friends when one of them cracked a hilarious joke and they all burst out laughing. 'X' was rocking backwards and forwards in a fit of hysterical laughter, when suddenly the old sword-wound burst open and his head fell to the ground in a pool of blood. His friends examined him, and this time he was well and truly dead.

His father decided to bring charges against the man who had told the joke. But the joker's friends collected some money together and succeeded in buying him off. The father buried his son and dropped the charges.

A Prank

A certain fellow of my home district, a well-known prank-
ster and libertine, was out one day strolling in the
countryside when he saw a young girl approaching on a
pony.

'I'll get a laugh out of her, see if I don't!' he called out
to his companions.

They were sceptical of his chances of success and
wagered a banquet on it, even as he hurried forward in
front of the girl's pony and cried out loudly, 'I want to
die! I want to die . . .'

He took hold of a tall millet stalk that was growing
over a nearby wall and, bending it so that it projected a
foot into the road, untied the sash of his gown and threw
it over the stalk, making a noose in it and slipping it
round his neck, as if to hang himself. As she came closer,
the girl laughed at him, and by now his friends were also
in fits. The girl then rode on into the distance, but the man
still did not move, which caused his friends to laugh all
the more. Presently they went up and looked at him: his

tongue was protruding from his mouth, his eyes were closed. He was quite lifeless.

Strange that a man could succeed in hanging himself from a millet stalk. Let this be a warning to libertines and pranksters.

King of the Nine Mountains

There was a certain gentleman by the name of Li from the town of Caozhou, an official scholar of the town, whose family had always been well off, though their residence had never been extensive. The garden behind their house, of an acre or two, had been largely abandoned.

One day, an old man arrived at the house, inquiring about a place to rent. He said he was willing to spend as much as a hundred taels, but Li declined, arguing that he had insufficient space.

'Please accept my offer,' pleaded the old man. 'I will cause you no trouble whatsoever.'

Li did not quite understand what he meant by this, but finally agreed to accept the money and see what happened.

A day later, the local people saw carriages and horses and a throng of people streaming into the garden behind Li's residence. They found it hard to believe that the place could accommodate so many, and asked Li what was going on. He himself was quite at a loss to explain, and hurried in to investigate, but found no trace of anything.

A few days later, the old man called on him again.

'I have enjoyed your hospitality already for several days and nights,' he said. 'Things have been very hectic. We have been so busy settling in, I am afraid we simply have not had time to entertain you as we should have done. Today I have asked my daughters to prepare a little meal, and I hope you will honour us with your presence.'

Li accepted the invitation and followed the old man into the garden, where this time he beheld a newly constructed range of most splendid and imposing buildings. They entered one of these, the interior of which was most elegantly appointed. Wine was being heated in a cauldron out on the verandah, while the delicate aroma of tea emanated from the kitchen. Presently wine and food were served, all of the finest quality and savour. Li could hear and see countless young people coming and going in the courtyard, and he heard the voices of girls chattering and laughing behind gauze curtains. Altogether he estimated that, including family and servants, there must have been over a thousand people living in the garden.

Li knew they must all be foxes. When the meal was finished, he returned home and secretly resolved to find a way of killing them. Every time he went to market he bought a quantity of saltpetre, until he had accumulated several hundred catties of the stuff, which he put down everywhere in the garden. He set light to it, and the flames leaped up into the night sky, spreading a cloud of smoke like a great black mushroom. The pungent odour of

35

the smoke and the choking particles of burning soot prevented anyone from getting close, and all that could be heard was the deafening din of a thousand screaming voices. When the fire had finally burned itself out and Li went into the garden, he saw the bodies of dead foxes lying everywhere, countless numbers of them, charred beyond recognition. He was still gazing at them when the old man came in from outside, an expression of utter devastation and grief on his face.

'What harm did we ever do you?' he reproached Li. 'We paid you a hundred taels – far more than it was worth – to rent your ruin of a garden. How could you be so cruel as to destroy every last member of my family? It is a terrible thing that you have done, and we will most certainly be revenged!'

And with those bitter words of anger, he took his leave.

Li was concerned that he would cause trouble. But a year went by without any strange or untoward occurrence.

It was the first year of the reign of the Manchu Emperor Shunzhi. There were hordes of bandits up in the hills, who formed huge roving companies which the authorities were quite powerless to apprehend. Li had numerous dependants and was especially concerned at the disturbances.

Then, one day, a fortune-teller arrived in the town, calling himself the Old Man of the Southern Mountain. He claimed to be able to see into the future with the utmost accuracy, and soon became something of a local

九山王

啸聚山林一念差
痴老人不是市
王師妻孥聯
残東郊日记
石囷中縱大時

'What harm did we ever do you?'

celebrity. Li sent for him and asked him to read his Eight Astrological Signs. The old man did so, and then rose hurriedly to his feet with a gesture of reverence.

'You, sir, are a true lord, an emperor among men!'

Li was flabbergasted and thought that perhaps the old man was making it all up. But he insisted that he was telling the truth, and Li was almost tempted to believe it himself.

'But I am a nobody,' he said. 'Tell me: when did a man ever receive the Mandate of Heaven and become Emperor in this way – with his own bare hands?'

'Why,' declared the old man, 'throughout history! Our Emperors have always come from the ranks of the common people. Which founder of a dynasty was ever *born* Son of Heaven?'

Now Li, who was beginning to get carried away, drew close to the fortune-teller and asked him for further guidance. The old man declared that he himself would be willing to serve as Li's Chief Marshal, just as the great wizard and strategist Zhuge Liang had once served the Pretender Liu Bei in the time of the Three Kingdoms. Li was to make ready large quantities of suits of armour and bows and crossbows. When Li expressed doubts that anyone would rally to his side, the old man replied, 'Allow me to work for you in the hills, sir. Let me forge links and win men over. Once word is out that you are indeed the true Son of Heaven, have no fear, the fighters of the hills will flock to you.'

Li was overjoyed, and instructed the old man to do as he proposed. He took out all the gold he had and gave orders for the necessary quantity of suits of armour to be made. Several days later, the old man was back.

'Thanks principally to Your Majesty's great aura of blessing, and in some negligible part to my own paltry abilities as an orator, on every hill the men are now thronging to join your cause and rallying to your banner.'

Sure enough, ten days later, a large body of men came in person to swear their allegiance to the new Son of Heaven and to the Old Man of the Southern Mountain whom they acknowledged as their Supreme Marshal. They set up a great standard, with a forest of brightly coloured pennants fluttering in the breeze, and from their stockade on one of the hills they lorded it over the region.

The District Magistrate led out a force to quell this rebellion, and the rebels under the command of the old fortune-teller inflicted a crushing defeat on the government troops. The Magistrate took fright and sent for urgent reinforcements from the Prefect. The Old Marshal harassed these fresh troops, ambushing and overwhelming them, killing large numbers, including several of their commanding officers. The rebels were now more widely feared than ever. They numbered ten thousand, and Li formally proclaimed himself the King of the Nine Mountains, while his Marshal was given the honorific title of Lord Marshal Protector of the Realm. The old man now reckoned his troops were short of horses, and since it so happened that the authorities in the capital were sending some horses under escort to the south, he dispatched some men to intercept the convoy and seize the horses. The success of this operation increased the prestige of the King of the Nine Mountains still further. He took his ease in his mountain lair, well satisfied with himself and considering it now merely a matter of time before he was officially installed on the Dragon Throne.

The Governor of Shandong Province now decided, mainly on account of the seizure of the horses, to launch a large-scale expedition to quell the rebellion once and for all. He received a report from the Prefect of Yanzhou, and sent large numbers of crack troops, who were to co-ordinate with detachments from the six local circuits and converge on the rebel stronghold from all sides. The King of the Nine Mountains became alarmed and summoned his Marshal for a strategic consultation, only to find that the old man had vanished. The 'King' was truly at his wits' end. He climbed to the top of one of the mountains of his 'domain' and looked down on the government forces and their standards, which stretched along every valley and on every hilltop.

'Now I see,' he declared sombrely, 'how great is the might of the Emperor's court!'

His stronghold was destroyed, the King himself was captured, his wife and entire family were executed. Only then did Li understand that the Marshal was the old fox, taking his revenge for the destruction of his own fox-family.

Butterfly

Luo Zifu was born in Bin County, and lost both his parents at an early age. When he was eight or nine years old he went to live with his Uncle Daye, a high official in the Imperial College and an immensely wealthy man. Daye had no sons of his own and came to love Luo as if he were his own child.

When the boy was fourteen, he fell in with bad company and became a regular frequenter of the local pleasure-houses. A famous Nanking courtesan happened to be in Bin County at the time, and the young Luo became hopelessly infatuated with her. When she returned to Nanking, he ran away with her and lived with her there in her establishment for a good six months – by which time his money was all gone and the other girls had begun to mock him mercilessly, though they still tolerated his presence.

Then he contracted syphilis and broke out in suppurating sores, which left stains on the bedding, and they finally drove him from the house. He took to begging in the streets, where the passers-by shunned him. He began to dread the thought of dying so far from home, and one

day set off begging his way back to Shaanxi, covering ten
or so miles a day, until eventually he came to the borders
of Bin County. His filthy rags and foul, pus-covered body
made him too ashamed to go any further into his old
neighbourhood, and instead he hobbled about on the
outskirts of town.

Towards evening, he was stumbling towards a temple
in the hills, seeking shelter for the night, when he encoun-
tered a young woman of a quite unearthly beauty, who
came up to him and asked him where he was going. He
told her his whole story.

'I myself have renounced the world,' was her response.
'I live here in a cave in the hills. You are welcome to stay
with me. Here at least you will be safe from tigers and
wolves.'

Luo followed her joyfully, and together they walked
deeper into the hills. Presently he found himself at the
entrance to a grotto, inside which flowed a stream, with
a stone bridge leading over it. A few steps further and
they came to two chambers hollowed out of the rock,
both of them brightly lit, but with no sign anywhere of
either candle or lamp. The girl bid Luo remove his rags
and bathe in the waters of the stream.

'Wash,' she said, 'and your sores will all be healed.'

She drew apart the bed-curtains and made up a bed for
him, dusting off the quilt.

'Sleep now,' she said, 'and I will make you a pair of
trousers.'

She brought in what looked like a large plantain leaf and began cutting it to shape. He lay there watching her, and in a very short while the trousers were made and placed folded on the bed.

'You can wear these in the morning.'

She lay down on a couch opposite.

After bathing in the stream, Luo felt all the pain go out of his sores, and when he awoke during the night and touched them, they had already dried and hardened into thick scabs. In the morning he rose, wondering if he would truly be able to wear the plantain-leaf trousers. When he took them in his hands, he found that they were wonderfully smooth, like green satin.

In a little while, breakfast was prepared. The young woman brought more leaves from the mountainside. She said that they were pancakes, and they ate them, and sure enough they were pancakes. She cut the shapes of poultry and fish from the leaves and cooked them, and they made a delicious meal. In the corner of the room stood a vat filled with fine wine, from which they drank, and when the supply ran out she merely replenished it with water from the stream.

In a few days, when all his sores and scabs were gone, he went up to her and begged her to share his bed.

'Silly boy!' she cried. 'No sooner cured than you go losing your head again!'

'I only want to repay your kindness . . .'

They had much pleasure together that night.

•

Time passed, and one day another young woman came into the grotto and greeted them with a broad grin.

'Why, my dear wicked little Butterfly!' (for such was the girl's name). 'You *do* seem to be having a good time! And when did this cosy little idyll of yours begin, pray?'

'It's been such an age since you last visited, dearest Sister Flower!' returned Butterfly, with a teasing smile. 'What Fair Wind of Love blows you here today? And have you had your little baby boy yet?'

'Actually I had a girl . . .'

'What a doll factory you are!' quipped Butterfly. 'Didn't you bring her with you?'

'She's only just this minute stopped crying and fallen asleep.'

Flower sat down with them and drank her fill of wine.

'This young man must have burned some very special incense to be so lucky,' she remarked, looking at Luo. He in turn studied her. She was a beautiful young woman in her early twenties, and the susceptible young man was instantly smitten. He peeled a fruit and 'accidentally' dropped it under the table. Bending down to retrieve it, he gave the tip of one of her tiny embroidered slippers a little pinch. She turned away and smiled, pretending not to have noticed. Luo, who was now totally entranced and more than a little aroused, noticed all of a sudden that his gown and trousers were growing cold, and when he looked down at them they had turned into withered leaves. Horrified, he sat primly upright for a moment, and slowly they reverted to their former soft, silken appearance. He was secretly relieved that neither of the girls seemed to have noticed anything.

A little later, they were still drinking together when he let his finger stray to the palm of Flower's dainty little hand. Flower carried on laughing and smiling, as if nothing had happened. And then suddenly, to his horror, it happened a second time: silk was transformed to leaf, and leaf back to silk. He had learned his lesson this time, and resolved to behave himself.

'Your young man is rather naughty!' said Flower, with a smile. 'If you weren't such a jealous jar of vinegar, he'd be roaming all over the place!'

'You faithless boy!' quipped Butterfly. 'You deserve to freeze to death!'

She and Flower both laughed and clapped their hands.

'My little girl's awake again,' said Flower, rising from her seat. 'She'll hurt herself crying like that.'

'Hark at you,' said Butterfly, 'leading strange men astray and neglecting your own child!' Flower left them, and Luo was afraid he would be subjected to mockery and recrimination from Butterfly. But she was as delightful as ever.

The days passed, and, as autumn turned to winter, the cold wind and frost stripped the trees bare. Butterfly gathered the fallen leaves and began storing them for food to see them through the winter. She noticed Luo shivering, and went to the entrance of the grotto, where she gathered white clouds with which to line a padded gown for him. When it was made, it was warm as silk, and the padding was light and soft as fresh cotton floss.

A year later, she gave birth to a son, a clever, handsome child with whom Luo loved to pass the days playing in the grotto. But, as time went by, he began to pine for home and begged Butterfly to return with him.

'I cannot go,' she told him. 'But you go if you must.'

A further two or three years went by. The boy grew, and they betrothed him to Flower's little daughter. Luo was now constantly thinking of his old uncle, Daye.

'The old man is strong and well,' Butterfly assured him. 'You do not need to worry on his behalf. Wait until your boy is married. Then you can go.'

She would sit in the grotto and write lessons on leaves for their son, who mastered them at a single glance.

'Our son has a happy destiny,' she said to Luo. 'If he goes into the human world, he will certainly rise to great heights.'

When the boy was fourteen, Flower came with her daughter, dressed in all her finery. She had grown into a radiantly beautiful young woman. She and Butterfly's son were very happy to be married, and the whole family held a feast to celebrate their union. Butterfly sang a song, tapping out the rhythm with her hairpin:

> A fine son have I,
> Why should I yearn

For pomp and splendour?
A fine daughter is mine,
Why should I long
For silken luxury?
Tonight we are gathered
To sing and be merry.
For you, dear lad, a parting cup!
For you, a plate of food!

Flower took her leave. The young couple made their home in the stone chamber opposite, and the young bride waited dutifully on Butterfly as if she were her own mother.

It was not long before Luo started talking again of returning home.

'You will always be a mortal,' said Butterfly. 'It is in your bones, and in our son's. He, too, belongs in the world of men. Take him with you. I do not wish to blight his days.'

The young bride wanted to say a last farewell to her mother, and Flower came to visit them. Both she and her husband were loth to leave their mothers, and their eyes brimmed with tears.

'Go for a while,' said the women, by way of comforting them. 'You can always come back later.'

Butterfly cut out a leaf and made a donkey, and the three of them, Luo and the young couple, climbed on to the beast and rode away upon it.

Luo's uncle, Daye, was by now an old man and retired from public life. He thought that his adopted son had died. And now, out of the blue, there he was, with a son of his own and a beautiful daughter-in-law! He rejoiced as if he had come upon some precious treasure. The moment they entered his house, their silken clothes all turned once more into crumbling plantain leaves, while the 'cotton padding' drifted up into the sky. They dressed themselves in new, more ordinary clothes.

As time went by, Luo pined for Butterfly, and he went in search of her with his son. But the path through the hills was strewn with yellow leaves, and the entrance to the grotto was lost in the mist. The two of them returned weeping from their quest.

The Black Beast

My friend's grandfather Li Jingyi once told the following story.

A certain gentleman was picnicking on a mountainside near the city of Shenyang when he looked down and saw a tiger come walking by, carrying something in its mouth. The tiger dug a hole and buried whatever it was in the ground. When he had gone, the gentleman told his men to find out what it was the tiger had buried. They came back to inform him that it was a deer, and he bade them retrieve the dead animal and fill up the hole.

Later the tiger returned, followed this time by a shaggy black beast. The tiger went in front as if it were politely escorting an esteemed guest. When the two animals reached the hole, the black beast squatted to one side and watched intently while the tiger felt in the earth with his paws, only to discover that the deer was no longer there. The tiger lay there prostrate and trembling, not daring to move. The black beast, thinking that the tiger had told a lie, flew into a fury and struck the tiger on the forehead with its paw. The tiger died immediately, and the black beast went away.

黑獸

鄭人葦庵克歲震山頴盛
涓一聲隊峰歧由来猛托
原不知此獸可能除 吳獸

The tiger returned, followed by a shaggy black beast.

The Stone Bowl

A certain gentleman by the name of Yin Tu'nan, of Wuchang, possessed a villa that he rented out to a young scholar. Half a year passed and he never once had occasion to call on this young tenant of his. Then one day he chanced to see him outside the entrance to the compound, and observing that, despite the tenant's evident youth, he had the fastidious manner and elegant accoutrements of a person of refinement, Yin approached him and engaged him in conversation. He found him indeed to be a most charming and cultivated person. Clearly this was no ordinary lodger.

Returning home, Yin mentioned the encounter to his wife, who sent over one of her own maids to spy out the land, on the pretext of delivering a gift. The maid discovered a young lady in the young man's apartment, of a breathtaking beauty that surpassed (as she put it) that of a fairy, while the living quarters, she observed to her mistress, were furnished with an extraordinary variety of plants, ornamental stones, rare clothes and assorted curios, things such as she had never before set eyes on.

Yin was intrigued to find out exactly what sort of person this young man could be, and went himself to the villa to pay him a visit. It so happened the man was out, but the following day he returned Yin's visit and presented his name card. Yin read on the card that his name was Yu De, but when Yin pressed Yu De for further details of his background, he became extremely vague.

'I am happy to make your acquaintance, sir. Trust me, I am no robber, nor am I a fugitive from justice. But beyond that, I am surely not obliged to divulge further particulars of my identity.'

Yin apologized for his incivility and set wine and food before his guest, whereupon they dined together in a most convivial manner until late in the evening, when two dark-skinned servants came with horses and lanterns to fetch their young master home.

The following day, he sent Yin a note inviting him over to the villa for a return visit. When Yin arrived, he observed that the walls of the room in which he was received were lined with a glossy paper that shone like the surface of a mirror, while fumes of some exotic incense smouldered from a golden censer fashioned in the shape of a lion. Beside the censer stood a vase of dark-green jade containing four feathers – two phoenix feathers, two peacock – each of them over two feet in length. In another vase, made of pure crystal, was a branch of some flowering tree which he could not identify, also about two feet long, covered with pink blossoms and trailing down over the edge of the little table on which it stood. The densely clustered flowers, still in bud, were admirably set off by the sparsity of leaves. They resembled butterflies moistened by the morning dew, resting with closed wings on the branch, to which they were attached by delicate antenna-like tendrils.

The dinner served consisted of eight dishes, each one a gastronomic delicacy. After dinner, the host ordered his servant to 'sound the drum for the flowers' and to commence the drinking game. The drum duly sounded, and as it did so the flowers on the branch began to open tremulously, spreading their 'butterfly wings' very slowly one by one. And then as the drumming ceased, on the final solemn beat, the tendrils of one flower detached themselves from the branch and became a butterfly, fluttering through the air and alighting on Yin's gown. With a laugh, Yu poured his guest a large goblet of wine, and when Yin had drained the goblet dry, the butterfly flew away. An instant later the drumming recommenced, and this time when it ceased two butterflies flew up into the air and settled on Yu's cap. He laughed again.

'Serves me right! I must drink a double sconce myself!'

And he downed two goblets. At the third drumming, a veritable shower of butterfly-flowers began to fall through the air, fluttering here and there and eventually settling in large numbers on the gowns of both men. The pageboy drummer smiled and thrust out his fingers twice, in the manner of drinking games: once for Yin, and it

came to nine fingers; once for Yu, and it came to four. Yin
was already somewhat the worse for drink and was unable
to down his quota. He managed to knock back three
goblets, and then got down from the table, excused himself and stumbled home. His evening's entertainment had
only served to intensify his curiosity. There was indeed
something very unusual about his lodger.

Yu seldom socialized, and spent most of his time shut
up at home in the villa, never going out into society even
for occasions such as funerals or weddings. Yin told his
friends of his own strange experience and word soon got
around, with the result that many of them competed to
make Yu's acquaintance, and the carriages of the local
nobility were often to be seen at the doors of the villa. Yu
found this attention more and more irksome, and one day
he suddenly took his leave of Yin and went away
altogether. After his departure, Yin inspected the villa
and found the interior of the building quite empty. It had
been left spotlessly clean and tidy. Outside, at the foot of
the stone steps leading up to the terrace, was a pile of
'candle tears', the waxen accumulation, no doubt, of the
revels of many evenings. Tattered curtains still hung in
the windows, and there seemed to be the marks of fingers
still visible on the fabric. Behind the villa, Yin found a
white stone bowl, about a gallon in capacity, which he
took home with him, filled with water and used for his
goldfish. A year later, he was surprised to see that the
water in the bowl was still as clear as it had been on the

very first day. Then, one day, a servant was moving a rock and accidentally broke a piece out of the rim of the bowl. But somehow, despite the break, the water stayed intact within the bowl, and when Yin examined it, it seemed to all intents and purposes whole. He passed his hand along the edge of the break, which felt strangely soft. When he put his hand inside the bowl, water came trickling out along the crack, but when he withdrew his hand, water filled the bowl as before.

Throughout the winter months, the water in the bowl never froze. And then one night it turned into a solid block of crystal. But the fish could still be seen swimming around inside it.

Yin was afraid that others might get to know of this strange bowl, and he kept it in a secret room, telling only his own children and their husbands and wives. But, with time, word got out and everyone was at his door wanting to see and touch this marvel.

The night before the festival of the winter solstice, the crystal block suddenly melted and water leaked from the bowl, leaving a large dark stain on the floor. Of the goldfish there was no sign whatsoever. Only the fragments of the broken bowl remained.

One day, a Taoist came knocking at the door and asked to see the bowl. Yin brought out the broken pieces to show him.

'This,' said the Taoist, 'was once a water vessel from the Dragon King's Underwater Palace.'

Yin told him how it had been broken, and how it had continued to hold water.

'That is the spirit of the bowl at work,' commented the Taoist, entreating Yin to give him a piece of it. Yin asked him why he wanted it.

'By pounding such a fragment into a powder,' he replied, 'I can make a drug that will give everlasting life.'

Yin gave him a piece, and the Taoist thanked him and went on his way.